WILD FOREVER
WILD HEART MOUNTAIN: WILD RIDERS MC
BOOK FIVE

SADIE KING

WILD FOREVER

His military training didn't prepare him for life as a single dad...

There was a surprise waiting for me when I got back from the military. A screaming, pooping, noisy surprise.

I'm a hard man, a biker who loves the quiet of the mountains. But my quiet life is shattered by the infant who's relying on me.

Her mother passed, and I'm all she has . . . until her aunt turns up trying to get custody of my baby.

April would be infuriating if she wasn't so hot.

But where was she when the baby needed her family? And why has she only just surfaced now?

Wild Forever is a single dad, found family, age gap romance featuring an ex-military biker mountain man and the curvy, innocent woman he makes his forever.

Copyright © 2023 by Sadie King.

All rights reserved.

No part of this book may be reproduced in any form or by any electronic or mechanical means, including information storage and retrieval systems, without written permission from the author, except for the use of brief quotations in a book review.

Cover designed by Cormer Covers.

This is a work of fiction. Any resemblance to actual events, companies, locales or persons living or dead, are entirely coincidental.

Please respect the author's hard work and do the right thing.

www.authorsadieking.com

CONTENTS

1. Grant — 1
2. April — 8
3. Grant — 12
4. April — 21
5. Grant — 30
6. April — 35
7. Grant — 43
8. April — 47
9. Grant — 56
10. Grant — 65
11. April — 69
    Epilogue — 77

Bonus Scene — 85
Wild Heart — 89
Books and Series by Sadie King — 97
About the Author — 99

1
GRANT

The wind whips at my beard and the sun warms my face as I ride down Sycamore Avenue, the main street in Hope. It's been a long time since I got out for a decent ride on my bike, and this afternoon has felt like freedom.

I stopped by to visit my old military buddy, Dylon, who lives on this side of the mountain, and he sent me home with a bag full of baby clothes that his little girl, Cleo, has grown out of.

My own daughter is at the Wild Riders MC clubhouse, where she spends three days a week in the care of the women there while I work.

But today I shut up shop and took my bike out for a solo ride.

It's the first time since my daughter, Bailey, arrived in my life three months ago that I've gotten out for a decent ride. I've enjoyed being on the road, but my chest hurts when I think about Bailey. I miss her.

There's a parking lot by the river on the outskirts of town, and I pull over and slide my phone out of my pocket. It'll be the last good place to stop before I take the mountain road over to Wild.

There's a missed call, and I grimace when I see it's from April.

I've never met the woman, but just seeing her name on my phone gives me a headache. It's probably another message explaining why she'd be better off with custody of her niece than me, the father.

The aunt wasn't around when Bailey's mother passed, and I got custody. I have no idea why April thinks she has a hope in hell now of claiming my daughter.

I delete the message without listening to it and push the thought of the persistent aunt out of my mind.

There's no message from Danni, who's minding Bailey, and I send her a quick text.

She replies instantly.

She's fine, Snips, same as she was half an hour ago.

. . .

I'm half relieved and half disappointed that my daughter is fine without me. I pocket the phone and am about to pull out onto the road that leads out of town and to the other side of the mountain when a thick, tanned leg catches my eye.

A woman leans against one of the large boulders by the river. Her shorts ride up, revealing her thick thighs. My eye travels up her legs to her wide waist and the lines of her breasts pushed against the black blouse with a large rose print that she's wearing.

My mouth goes dry at the sight of her. She's gorgeous.

Long dark hair falls over her shoulders and frames her heart-shaped face. Her lips are pink and plump, her cheekbones round like two rosy apples. I can't see the color of her eyes from this distance, but there are dark smudges under them and a crease on her brow.

Gorgeous but troubled.

She's breathing hard like she's just sat down after exertion and her chest rises and falls dramatically, each breath causing her breasts to push outward so that her cleavage expands enticingly.

My breath catches in my chest as I forget to breathe, and my phone slips out of my hand.

"Shit," I mutter as I fumble to catch it before it hits the gravel.

When I look up the woman has arched her back, rubbing the base of her spine with her face set in a grimace. She looks like she's in pain.

I roll my bike over to where she is, and her eyes follow me warily. They're hazel, and as her gaze sweeps over my body, I feel the heat of it. My skin prickles, and it's lucky I'm straddling a bike or she'd see me harden through my leathers.

She's the most beautiful creature I've ever seen, and for a moment I can't speak. We look at each other, and I swear energy crackles in the air between us. My hearing goes muffled, my skin prickles, and a surge of energy races through my veins.

I have the distinct feeling that this is a life-changing moment. My life will be divided into the days before I saw this woman and the days after.

Mine.

The word springs into my head and settles into my heart. This woman is mine, whoever she is. She's my future, my everything…

"Can I help you?"

I'm brought down to earth by her suspicious tone.

The woman crosses her arms across her chest and glances around us. I don't blame her. I'm a hairy bastard on a huge Harley with an MC patch on my leather jacket, and I've been staring at her, dumbstruck, for the last minute.

I hold my hands up in the universal gesture showing her that I mean no harm.

"I'm Snips." I don't realize I've given her my road name until her eyes narrow suspiciously. "I mean Grant. I'm Grant."

I'm fumbling like a damn fool, but this woman has got my tongue tied all up in knots.

"Which is it, Snips or Grant?" There's a smile in her eyes, but she's still wary.

"Both. Snips is my road name, but you can call me Grant."

She doesn't offer her name, but she seems to relax a little. She rubs her lower back, and I'm reminded of why I came over in the first place.

"You look like you're in pain. Do you need help?"

She shakes her head. "It's an old injury. It acts up sometimes, that's all."

She arches her back in a stretch that pushes her chest out. My gaze dips to her breasts, straining against her blouse so hard that the top button is about to pop undone. What I wouldn't give to rip that button open…

"Do you know if there's a bus to Wild?"

My attention snaps back to her face, and she's

looking at me pointedly. I'm totally busted staring at her chest, but when her breasts are so luscious, it's hard not to.

My gaze settles on her eyes, which are flecked with golden amber.

"Umm..." Jesus, I've never stuttered in my life, but this girl has me behaving like a teenager with a crush, not a fully grown man.

I clear my throat, trying to regain control of myself.

"There's a bus twice a day at ten and two."

She glances at her phone and swears under her breath.

"I knew I shouldn't have stopped at Babyland."

She's got a branded shopping bag by her side and a small backpack leaning against the boulder. If I squeezed everything up, I could just fit it in my saddle bag.

"I'm going to Wild; I'll give you a lift."

She eyes me skeptically, but I detect curiosity behind the barrier she's put up. I don't blame her for holding back. I'm a stranger on a bike. I wouldn't accept a lift from me either. But if she's going to Wild and I'm going to Wild... it seems like fate to me.

I slide off my bike and open my saddle bag.

"I've got room in here for your things."

I pull out the plastic bag of baby clothes that Dylon gave me, and a pink dress falls in the gravel.

"I'll refold these so there's more room."

"You've got a little girl?" She eyes the pink dress with curiosity.

"It's too small to be mine," I say.

She smiles for the first time, and I catch my breath. If I thought she was beautiful before, she's stunning when she smiles. For a brief moment, the suspicion and the wariness fall away, and she's radiant. Youthful and carefree.

But it's gone in a moment.

"They're my daughter's."

The fact that I've got a kid seems to relax her, and I get it. I'm not a weird stranger anymore. I'm a dad, and I must be responsible.

"If it makes you feel any better, take a picture of me and the bike and send it to someone so they know who you got a lift with."

The smile drops off her face.

"I don't have anyone to send it to," she mutters as she pockets her phone.

Sadness flashes across her features, and then it's replaced by the wariness.

I want to smooth her brow, find out what's got her so down and then fix it. And most of all, I want to make her smile again.

2
APRIL

The stranger, Grant, smiles too much. It peeps through his beard and lights up his pale blue eyes, and every time he does it, I feel a twinge in my core.

Which is the last thing I need right now.

I'm on a mission, and there's no time to get distracted by a hot man in leather straddling a bike.

Not even one that has a tattoo peeping out from the top of his t-shirt that clings to his muscular chest under his jacket.

He's got red flags all over him, the kind of guy my caseworker would tell me to steer clear of. But like a fool, I'm contemplating his offer for a lift.

But what choice do I have?

I messed up the train timings and got to Hope late. Then I stupidly went for a walk along the river instead of waiting for the bus. But my back ached and needed a stretch, and now it still aches and needs a rest.

My fingers itch, and I scape them against my jeans.

Visualize your happy place.

I hear my therapist's voice in my head. It's her solution for when anything gets complicated.

With this bearded biker looking at me with intense curiosity and heat in his gaze, I think I just found my new happy place.

"Are you visiting someone in Wild?" he asks.

It's a fair question, but I'm not sure how to answer it. "I'm on vacation."

Which isn't exactly a lie.

He stares at me, this time managing to keep his gaze from my chest. Although I have to admit, I don't mind him checking me out.

My cheeks heat as he watches me. I'm not used to being looked at like this, like I'm somebody worth looking at.

"Most people stay in Hope. It's got the river and the shops. Why Wild? It's a bit off the beaten track."

Damn, he's asking too many questions. I stand up off the boulder, clenching my teeth when my back bites. It's been good lately, but six hours on a train has triggered the old pain.

"I like being off the beaten track."

I reach for my bag, hoping he gets the hint and doesn't ask any more questions, but before I get my backpack, he gets there first. Our fingers brush, and a spark of electricity jumps between us. It makes me gasp and I pull my hand back quickly, my eyes darting to his. He looks as shocked as I do, so he must have felt it too.

I turn away quickly. The last thing I need is to finally find a man I'm attracted to. Not here, not now.

He stuffs my bag into his saddle bag and takes the shopping bag as well. He looks at the Babyland bag and I can tell he's about to ask questions, so I cut him off.

"Do you know the Wild Times Hotel in Wild?"

"It's the only hotel in town." He frowns. "It's above the bar. Not a nice place for a girl like you."

I fold my arms and study him. He has no idea what kind of girl I am, but I appreciate the concern. Maybe a little too much.

"Get on, and I'll take you there."

He pulls the helmet off his head and slides it onto mine. His fingers adjust the catch, and when his fingertips brush my skin, heat skitters across my body and my pulse ramps up a notch.

His eyes meet mine, and there's a mischievous

glint to them as if he knows exactly what effect he's having on me.

"I didn't catch your name?"

There's no way I'm giving out my name, not until I get what I came for. I match his grin, going for a flirty tone.

"I don't give out my name to strangers."

It doesn't quite come out as lighthearted as I intended, but he chuckles anyway, and I'm relieved when he doesn't press me.

"You been on a bike before?"

I nod, and he frowns. Is that jealousy I see flash across his features? In a moment it's gone, and the jovial smile is back. I must have imagined it.

"Hold onto me and enjoy the view."

We peel out of the overlook lot and onto the road that heads out of town and into the mountains. I cling to his waist, breathing in the heady scent of leather and mountain pine.

I must be crazy. I know I'm crazy. This entire scheme of mine is crazy, the act of a desperate woman. I don't think I was thinking straight when I left home this morning.

But as I cling onto Grant, my head feels clear. Whatever happens this weekend, at least I got a ride on a motorbike behind a hot biker.

3
GRANT

There's only one thing better than riding a bike on the mountain road, and that's riding a bike on the mountain road with a gorgeous woman behind me.

The stranger is full of secrets. She hasn't even told me her name, but the press of her body against mine as we swerve around the corners is all I need to know she's mine. Her breasts brush up against my back, giving me a permanent hard-on.

I'm full of questions about who she is and why she's here, but for now I'll let her keep her secrets to herself. If I push her she might retreat, and I don't want that.

We pull up outside Wild Times Hotel & Bar, the only bar in town with a few rooms to rent above it. It's the middle of the afternoon, and there's loud music coming from inside and the sound of male laughter.

There is no way I'm letting this woman stay here. But if I take off back to my place, she might freak out. She seems flighty enough as it is, and I don't want to scare her. I need to make her see for herself how unsuitable this place is.

I park my bike out front, hoping none of the drunk clientele are stupid enough to touch her. I glare at the men who eye us warily as we dismount.

There are a few I recognize, local men who work at the sawmill.

"Shouldn't you be at work?" I ask John, a man in a wide hat with a red face who I recognize as one of the foremen at the mill. I cut most the men's hair in Wild and get to know everyone's business.

"Closed for maintenance."

Well, that explains why it's so busy in here today. He gives us a lopsided smile. "Join us for a drink?"

He holds up his empty glass, and I shake my head. "No thanks."

His gaze slides to the woman and I step in front of her protectively, my arm going around her shoulder.

She startles at my touch and warmth spreads up my arm. But she doesn't move away. I guess she sees the sense in sticking close to me when there are a bunch of men day drinking.

We maneuver past the outdoor tables and to the front desk. The place smells like sour beer and burgers.

There's a pool table in the corner, and a group of men stand around it with drinks in hand.

They look up as we come in, and one by one their gazes sweep over the woman like they haven't seen one before. And I get it; the sawmill is the main source of employment on this side of the mountain. There aren't a lot of women in town. But their attention makes my blood boil and I tighten my grip on her shoulder, letting them know she's mine.

"Ow." She gives me a sharp look. "You're squeezing me too tight."

But there's a hint of a smile on her lips. She's enjoying having my arm around her, and that makes me smile right back at her.

I loosen my grip, but only a little.

The woman scans the inside of the bar, and she can't hide her displeasure.

"This is the hotel?"

"The rooms are upstairs."

She squirms uncomfortably, and I don't blame her. I wouldn't want to stay in a place called Wild Times either.

"I'm not gonna let you stay here."

She narrows her eyes at me. "Not going to let me?"

"No. I wouldn't let my worst enemy stay here on a good day and especially not a woman alone when half the guys from the lumber yard are in there getting smashed."

"I can look after myself."

She folds her arms across her body, and I wonder where she learned to be so defensive. I want to peel the layers back and get to the softness inside.

"I'm sure you can. But you don't have to."

Not when I'm here to look after her. But if I admit what I'm feeling, she'll freak the fuck out.

A squat man with rosy red cheeks comes over to us.

"Hey Grant, what can I get you?"

"We're not here to drink, Hank."

"I'm looking for a room," the woman cuts in quickly, giving me a pointed look. Well, she is determined. If she insists on staying in this shithole, I'll just have to station myself outside the door all night.

Hank slides a lined notebook over from the desk and peers at the names written there. "You got a reservation?"

The woman's face falls. "No, I didn't think I'd need one."

Hank shakes his head. "Sorry hon, we're fully booked."

I could kiss Hank right now, but I keep my expression neutral as I lean on the bar. Something sticky tugs at my jacket, and I straighten up. This place needs a good clean.

"I got a spare room at my place."

The woman glances at me, her troubled eyes peeping out from under her bangs.

"Is there nowhere else?" Her face falls when she realizes what she's just said. "I mean, it's nice of you to offer, but you've already given me a lift. I can't put you out."

There're some cute B&Bs in town and cabins to rent, and plenty of people rent out spare rooms in their houses, but I'm not going to tell this beauty that.

"You're not putting me out. You need a room, and I have one. Come on."

I head for the door, and she hesitates. "I'm not gonna harm you. Ask Hank here. Am I a decent man, Hank?"

Hank nods. "So decent I never see him in here."

The woman stares at me for a long time making her decision. I like her eyes on me and I guess I measure up, because she finally nods.

"I hope I don't regret this," she mutters as we head out of the bar.

I hope she doesn't regret this either. But there's no way I'm letting her stay anywhere other than my place. I want to keep her close to me. I want to get to know her, to know all her secrets.

I live in a cabin not far from the small town of Wild. It's halfway between my barbershop in town and the Wild Riders HQ which is further up the mountain. The two places I spend most of my time.

We ride to my place, and I pull the bike up and park it alongside the sensible Kia I bought when I realized I had a daughter.

The woman takes in the baby seat in the back and the wooden slide set out in front of the house.

"How old's your daughter?"

The mention of Bailey makes me smile. "My little girl's sixteen months old."

"Is, um, her mom okay with me staying here?"

There's uncertainty in her voice, and I'm pleased to detect a note of jealousy.

"Her mom's not around," is the simple answer I give her.

I only knew Karen for a weekend when I was on military leave. Being sent to war made me wild and reckless. It was a way to hide my fear that I might never come back, to spend my leave losing myself in drink and a woman.

When you don't know if the next time you'll be on American soil it will be in a body bag, you live every moment like it's your last. At least I did for a time.

It was only when Karen passed away in an accident four months ago that I found out Bailey existed. A paternity test proved what Karen had put on the birth certificate.

I hardly knew her mother apart from one wild weekend, but my daughter is my life. In four short months, she's taken over my heart.

I've not looked at a woman since I became a dad, but now that there's one before me, it feels different. I'm not looking for a cheap thrill anymore. I want to build a family for Bailey. If I get involved with anyone now, it will be for the long term.

But I don't tell the woman in front of me any of that as I let her into my house.

The living room is cluttered with baby gear. Bailey's colorful play mat is on the carpet littered with wooden toys and her favorite books, the corners worn from where she likes to suck on them. No matter how many chew toys I've bought her, she prefers the edges of books for some reason.

The woman looks around the space, taking it all in, and I wonder if she's having second thoughts.

"Don't worry, she's a good sleeper," I say. "Sleeps right through the night now."

She didn't when I first brought her home.

I drove to Huntington in West Virginia once I knew Bailey existed and collected her from the foster family she'd been staying with since Karen's accident. I spent a week staying in Huntington getting Bailey used to me and learning everything I could about looking after a baby from the kind foster parents before bundling her into the car and taking her home.

The poor thing must have missed her mom, and for the first two months she slept in the room with me. It's been a slow process getting her comfortable enough to sleep on her own. But finally I moved her into her own room down the hall.

I move around the living room picking up baby toys and doing a quick tidy up. I didn't expect company, and it's amazing how quickly the house gets cluttered when you've got a daughter who's just started walking.

The woman dumps her bags by the couch and squints at a photo on the wall. It's me and Bailey. She's smiling at the camera and holding out a tubby fist.

The woman startles and steps closer to examine the photo.

"How old did you say your daughter was again?"

If I wasn't so busy picking up stacking cups, I might have noticed the edge to her voice, but I don't.

"Sixteen months."

"And what's her name?"

Her voice sounds choked, and it makes me glance up at her. The woman's staring intently at the photo.

"Bailey."

"Bailey." The woman repeats the name in an odd tone.

I still don't know her name. It was a fun game when we were strangers, but if she's going to stay in my house, I need to know what to call her.

"And what was your name? You never told me."

The woman turns slowly with an odd expression on her face that I can't read. She pulls herself upright and stares me straight in the eye.

"April."

My heart drops at the name, and realization hits us at the same time.

She's April.

The strange, beautiful woman who's making my tummy flip and my dick hard is April, Bailey's lost aunt who's trying to get custody of my daughter.

April is right here in my house.

4
APRIL

My mouth drops open as realization hits me.

This is the guy. The sperm donor for my niece who's calling himself her father, when all he did was spend one wild weekend with my sister. He wasn't there through her pregnancy, he wasn't there when she gave birth or for the first year of Bailey's life, and now he thinks he can claim Bailey as his daughter.

Neither were you, a voice inside me whispers, and guilt floods me. I push it down because that's not the point right now.

The hot biker I've been salivating over for the last hour is the guy who's got the one thing in the world that I want. My niece. The last remaining family I have. Without Bailey, I'm all alone in this world.

"You," I whisper, "You're Bailey's father."

His face sets in a grim line. The cheerful, relaxed guy from earlier disappears behind a mask of steel, and I regret the loss.

"You're Bailey's aunt. The one who's been calling me and threatening to get custody."

I nod, because he's not wrong. I want my niece, and I'll do whatever it takes to get her.

We stare at each other for a long time, and damn if he isn't still the hottest man I've ever seen.

I push the thought aside.

He's the man standing in the way of me and my niece. It doesn't matter how much my body trembles with heat every time he brushes against me.

"Why are you here, April?"

His voice is hard, and I don't blame him. It doesn't look good turning up here, but I didn't have many other choices.

"I came to talk."

He folds his arms across his chest.

"Then talk."

It comes out as a growl that makes my knees go weak.

Damn him. I've spent weeks rehearsing this moment, and now all I can think about is what it would feel like if those strong arms had me pinned to a bed.

My palms sweat, and I wipe them on my shorts.

"I just want to see my niece. She's the only family I've got left. I thought if I came here and found you…"

I thought what? That if I explained my fucked up situation to him in person instead of letting him find out through the courts that he'd have some kind of empathy for me? That he'd see how devoted an aunt I am and hand over my niece? That I was hoping I'd find a man struggling to be a dad who'd be happy to hand over the baby to someone else?

But the way he's looking at me with his gaze hard makes my heart sink.

It was stupid to think I could walk into town, find Bailey, and convince her dad that his daughter was better off with me.

"I just want to see my niece," I say. "I miss her."

His gaze softens, but he keeps his arms folded. "Why now? Where were you when her mother died?"

I wince at his question and look away.

I've just spent a carefree hour with this man. We laughed together, and he made me feel things I haven't felt in a long time. He looked at me like I was someone worth looking at, someone desirable even. Not scum, not a lowlife, and not someone to be pitied. But as soon as he knows the truth about me, that will change. He won't look at me like a hungry man eyeing a juicy steak anymore, and he certainly won't let me near his daughter.

"I was sick." It's a half truth. Some call it a sickness.

His eyes narrow. "I didn't know Bailey existed. I never would have known if Karen hadn't passed. You could have taken custody, and I'd have been none the wiser."

"I couldn't," I mumble. "I wasn't in a position to."

The state wouldn't let me is closer to the truth, and I thank them for their privacy laws that stop them from telling Grant the entire truth, because if they had, he wouldn't still be here talking to me.

Grant's still staring at me like I'm his mortal enemy, and I don't blame him. It must look like I hijacked him in his own home, which is more or less what I planned to do.

The sound of a car pulling up outside has him frowning.

"Shit."

He runs a hand through his shaggy hair, and I glance outside.

A vintage caddy pulls up out front. It's a beautiful car with sleek edges and entirely out of place on the gravel drive of this cabin surrounded by woods.

There's a baby seat in the back, and my heart leaps.

"Is that Bailey?" I say excitedly.

"Yes," Grant grunts.

I stride to the window and then stop. "Is it okay if I see her?"

It seems a little too late to ask. I came to Wild because I found out that's where she was. I planned to walk the streets until I found her.

"It's not okay. None of this is okay, April." He runs a hand through his hair, a hand that sent heat through my body only a short time ago.

"I don't like it that you turned up here. You should have called."

My mouth drops open, because I tried to call him several hundred times.

"You could have picked up your phone. I left you messages."

He grunts again, and I know I'm right.

"I didn't think you were going to just turn up."

I fold my arms across my chest as anger simmers in my bones. "She's my niece, Grant. I'm entitled to see her."

Well, not technically. The courts said I can't see her, but that was when I was sick. I'm better now. I just can't afford the lawyer to make it official.

A woman gets out of the car and opens the back seat. There are two baby seats in there, and she unbuckles one and takes the cutest little girl out.

Her hair is dark and curly, just like Karen's, and her smile is as mischievous, which is always what was getting Karen into trouble. My sister loved the wild life. She was wild, good-natured, fun, and pretty, a lethal combination for attracting men.

My eyes shine as I think about Karen, and I wipe a tear away.

I catch Grant looking at me, and his expression softens.

"I don't like that you're here," he says. "But since you are, you can see your niece."

My heart soars, and before I know what I'm doing I throw my arms around him. Grant's as solid as the mighty trees that cover the mountain. He smells like baby milk and pine needles and beard oil, and it's so distinctive that I want to bury my nose in his shoulder and breathe him in.

But it's a stiff hug from his side, and I pull myself back before I embarrass myself by doing something stupid like sniffing him.

"Thank you," I say.

"But you can't stay here." His voice is firm, and my good feeling evaporates.

Whatever connection me and Grant had going on, it's been severed. He's the father now, protecting his daughter, and it breaks my heart that the thing he's protecting her from is me.

There's a knock at the door, and it opens before Grant reaches it.

"Hey, princess."

Bailey holds out her arms when she sees Grant and giggles. "Dadda," she says, and my heart breaks. She's talking now, and I missed it.

I missed all of it. The walking, the talking, her first smile. I wasn't there for any of it. Grant's right; what right do I have to be here now?

But all my doubts evaporate as I watch my niece, her easy smile and intelligent eyes as she tugs on Grant's beard.

"She went down after lunch for two hours," the woman says. She gives Grant a rundown on Bailey's day and is about to leave when Grant stops her.

"Are you going back to HQ, Danni?"

"Yeah," the woman says. "I need to close up the shop before I head home."

He glances at me, and the woman looks inside for the first time. Her gaze meets mine, and she smiles.

"I didn't know you had company." She raises an eyebrow at Grant, and he shakes his head with a scowl.

"She's not staying," Grant says. "This is April, and she needs a bed for the night. Can you drop her at the clubhouse? I'll call ahead and let the Prez know."

I look between them with my heart sinking fast.

I'm this close to my niece, but I've not been able to even touch her yet, and now I'm being sent away.

"It's safe there," says Grant. "There are rooms upstairs. You can get something to eat and stay the night, and I'll drop you back in Hope tomorrow."

He's going to drop me back tomorrow. I stare at him, my heart heavy. All this was for nothing. But what did I expect? That he would just hand Bailey over?

Well, yeah. I hoped the new dad would be happy to hand over his burden. I didn't expect to find a devoted father.

I hang my head because what choice do I have.

"Can't I just spend some time with her first? Tomorrow morning?"

Grant stares at me long and hard, and in that look I see a spark of the connection we shared earlier, before he knew who I was.

"I'll think about it."

It's the best I'm going to get out of him. Bailey's pulling at his beard and Danni's looking between us, probably wondering what the hell is going on but too polite to ask.

I grab my backpack and the fairy outfit I picked up for Bailey earlier.

"Here." I hand him the Babyland shopping bag. "It's a gift for my niece. I hope she likes it."

Bailey grabs for the handles of the bag, and Grant takes it from me.

"Thank you." It's hard for him to say the words, but he manages to choke them out. "I'll call HQ, but if you have any problems you call me."

"Will you pick up your phone?"

A ghost of a smile appears on his lips before he remembers to be cross with me. But that smile gives me hope.

Maybe Grant will be different from every other judgy person I've ever come across. Maybe if I told him the truth, he'd let me have access to my niece. To give me some connection to the only family I've got left.

5
GRANT

Bailey fusses as I rub the towel too harshly over her, wiping up water droplets from her bath.

"Sorry princess."

I lay her down on the towel and blow a raspberry on her tummy. She lets out a halfhearted giggle.

My little girl senses something's off. It has been ever since the revelation that her aunt was here in my house. The woman I'd been fantasizing about and was ready to share my heart with.

A pang of regret tugs at my chest.

I've never been attracted to anyone the way I was to April. It was more than attraction. The first time I laid eyes on her, my chest tightened with longing. When we stopped at the Wild Times bar and every man in the place cast his eyes on her, I was ready to punch every single one of them in the face for looking at her. A wave of possessiveness washed over me, and it hasn't fully left.

I sent April away to the clubhouse because she needed a place to stay, but I've been brooding about who she might meet there.

I called the Prez and then Travis, who runs the bar and restaurant, to let him know she was coming and she had the club's protection. He snickered at me until I told him who she was.

The entire club knows about my struggles with Bailey and the mysterious aunt who's suddenly claiming custody.

But I asked him to be respectful, and he will. He'll give her a free dinner and a room upstairs. Travis only has eyes for his new wife, Kendra, but I don't know who else is in tonight. My fingers drum on the tiled bathroom floor as I imagine one of my MC brothers hitting on her.

Arlo's hooked up with Maggie now, but Davis, the prospect who sometimes works the bar, is probably about the same age as April. Then there's Quentin, the brooding manager of the brewery.

There's a snapping noise, and I'm surprised to find one of Bailey's plastic bath toys snapped in my fist.

She looks at the plastic crocodile with its head hanging askew and lets out a wail.

"Shhh. I'll buy you a new one."

I dump the broken crocodile in the trash, and her cries get louder.

I pick my daughter up and pull her close. Her little hands beat against my shoulder. She's really not happy tonight, and I'm sure it's my fault. Her damn aunt has me all shook up.

My thoughts swing between imagining her thighs wrapped around me and imaging showing her out of town. It's enough to give a man whiplash.

"Croco," Bailey wails, her hand reaching for the trash.

"Here, honey, have the octopus instead."

I hand her the purple octopus, and she takes it sullenly. But it does the trick, and she's distracted enough to let me get her diaper and onesie on with no complaints.

I sing the bananas in pajamas song to her as I do up the pop buttons, and she giggles. Her smile warms all the cold places of my heart.

I'm blessed to have Bailey in my life, and I can't imagine what I'd do if someone took her off me. Maybe that's how April feels. She said Bailey is her last remaining family. Am I really going to withhold her access to that?

But where was she when Karen had the accident? Why didn't she claim Bailey then? The authorities tracked me down because Karen had named me on the birth certificate. Thank God for that, or I never would have known about my sweet daughter.

The thought makes me hug her close, and she squirms in my arms.

"You want your bottle?"

I grab the pre-heated bottle and take her through to the bedroom, laying her in the crib gently and handing her the bottle. She snatches it off me and sucks hungrily as I pull the blanket up around her.

Is it unfair not to let April see her? She's come all this way. The least I even do is hear her out and give her a chance to explain herself.

Since Bailey came into my life, I've had my barbershop open only three days a week. Danni and Trish help with the babysitting, and I've become close to the wives of my MC brothers. They've been the best source of help with minor coughs and tips for sleeping. We've got a text chain, and I message them if I have a question.

I'm not the only one in the club to have a baby, and I'm thankful for the support.

But once a week I close the doors to my barbershop and spend the day with just me and Bailey. Tomorrow is that day, and I'd planned to take her out in the baby backpack for a hike and a picnic. It can't hurt to invite April along.

"You want to see your aunt?"

Bailey gurgles, but the milk is making her sleepy. Even as she grasps the bottle, her eyes are drooping.

Once I've made the decision to invite April to spend the day with us, my heart feels lighter. The thought of seeing the curvy girl with the troubled eyes has my heart singing in a way it shouldn't. It's bad news to feel like this about the woman who's trying to take my baby away from me. Let alone the fact that she's my daughter's aunt and definitely off limits.

But the heart wants what the heart wants, and there's no denying the thought of spending a day with April is a pleasing one.

I watch Bailey for a long time until her mouth slackens and her breathing gets regular. Only then do I slip the bottle out of her grasp and sneak out of the room.

6
APRIL

*L*ater that night, I lie in bed thinking about the complicated man in a MC club who's become an instant father. He has every reason to be wary of me, but he's been nothing but thoughtful by sending me to the Wild Riders HQ.

Travis, who runs the bar, met me, and his wife Kendra took me under her wing, showing me to a room upstairs and making sure I got something to eat from the restaurant. Travis wouldn't take any money for the food or the room, and I guess I've got Grant to thank for that.

Kendra told me the club members are all army veterans who like to ride. They do charity runs and help out on community projects.

The members I met were welcoming and the women friendly. Maggie works in the kitchen, and she insisted I try a new dessert she's experimenting with.

I helped clear tables in the restaurant and fold napkins, trying to do something helpful to pay my way. It felt good to be there, like it's a big family.

One that I'm not a part of.

Loneliness settles into my bones as I stare at the patterns on the ceiling in the strange room.

We lost our parents when we were young, and I don't think I ever got over the trauma. I learned to acknowledge that with the help of my therapist.

Trauma manifests itself in different ways. For Karen, it was being carefree with her body. For me, well, it got me into the situation I'm in: deemed unfit to be guardian of my own niece.

A hollowness gnaws at my chest, and my fingers itch to relieve it some way. I close my eyes and suck in deep breaths as I count, the way I learned to do at the clinic.

In a few minutes, I'm calm again and in control.

My thoughts drift to the bearded man with the kind eyes and mischievous smile. As sleep claims me, I think about his arm around me, his searching eyes, and his scent which permeates my dreams.

. . .

The next morning, I'm waiting outside when Grant pulls up in his Kia. He called earlier, inviting me to spend the day with him and Bailey. I'm beyond relieved that he's giving me a chance, and I'm determined not to fuck it up.

Bailey's sleeping in the car seat and I get into the passenger side and close the door quietly, trying not to wake her.

"Don't worry," he assures me. "Once she's out, she's out. She won't wake now until she's ready."

I turn in my seat to look at my niece. Her little head rests on the back of the car seat and her mouth parts, letting out gentle snores.

"She's adorable."

Grant grunts, and a smile tugs on his lips.

"She is."

We drive further up the mountain, and he pulls onto a gravel road that leads to a parking lot and the start of hiking trails.

"I hope you bought your walking shoes."

He turns off the engine and checks Bailey in the rearview mirror. She's still sleeping.

"Do we wake her?"

"Noooo." He shakes his head emphatically. "Never wake a sleeping baby. She'll wake on her own soon. Then we'll have a couple of hours to walk and picnic before I need to get her home for her afternoon nap."

I'm impressed by his schedule; he really knows what he's doing.

"So what do we do?"

He adjusts his seat so it leans back. "We wait." He turns to me, and I get the full effect of his intense gaze. "And while we wait for her to wake up, you can tell me exactly why you're here and why the sudden interest in your niece."

I try not to let it show how much his words dismay me. I was hoping we'd get the day together first before I had to tell him the truth.

I choose my words carefully. "I thought if we talked face to face, we might be able to work something out."

He nods. "That makes sense. I haven't been easy to get a hold of."

I'm surprised he's admitting that, and it shows he's prepared to be reasonable. "Why didn't you answer my calls?"

His brow furrows. "Because I thought you were trying to take my daughter away from me."

I look away because I kind of was, but now that I've seen them together, I know how impossible that is. The best I can hope for now is to have my niece in my life somehow, but it's clear to me her father won't be giving her up.

I search my heart and find that I'm okay with that.

"The truth is, I didn't know what kind of a man you were," I say honestly. "My sister…"

I pause, not wanting to speak ill of the dead. I love my sister and I'm not judging her choices, but… "My sister had a wild side."

Grant nods. "I know."

A flash of jealousy rages through my veins. My sister was in Grant's arms. He pinned her down, not me. He kissed her and… I squeeze my eyes shut tight, not wanting to think about what they must have done together.

"Are you okay?" he asks.

"Yeah, I just…I can't imagine you with Karen."

He stares out at the forest, and something like regret slides over his face.

"I was in a dark place when I met your sister. I was in the military for twelve years."

I'm not surprised by his admission. He gives off the aura of a military man, strong and capable and organized.

"Sometimes when I came back, all I wanted was to forget where I'd been. Karen helped me forget."

"Did you love her?" I hope he doesn't hear the tightness in my voice.

He shakes his head. "Love didn't come into it." He runs a hand over his hair. "That was over two years ago. I've changed since then."

He gives me a look that's tinged with regret, and I remember the connection we had yesterday, what this might have been if the circumstances were different.

"I'm sorry about your sister," he says gently.

"Thanks." I sigh, and sadness washes over me like it does when I think about Karen. We weren't close the last few years, and I regret that more than anything.

"So, you wanted to make sure I wasn't some sketchy low life who'd hooked up with your sister?"

Grant smiles, and I'm relieved that his good humor is back.

"Yeah, that's about right."

"And am I?"

He's far from what I expected. He's got a business and a MC club that's like extended family, a cabin in the woods, and beautiful mountain trails on his doorstep. Bailey will have a good life here, and the realization hurts my heart. She's better off here than with me.

"So why now? Where were you when Karen had the accident and Bailey needed family?"

It's the question I've been dreading, and I'm still not sure how to answer it. I run my sweaty palm along my shorts and take a deep breath.

"I was sick." It's kind of the truth. "I was in a clinic, and I wasn't deemed well enough to be Bailey's guardian."

He peers at me for a long time.

"Mental health issues can do that," he says quietly. "I've seen it with some of the men who I served with."

It's not a big leap for him to go there, and I'm about to correct him. It wasn't a mental health issue, not in the traditional sense, although my therapist made me see that my childhood trauma had something to do with it.

Grant rests a hand on my leg. It's supposed to be comforting, but the heat causes my whole body to come alive.

"It's nothing to be ashamed of, April."

I stare at him and I should correct his assumption, but the look of empathy in his eyes and the hand on my leg has my mouth staying firmly shut.

He thinks I was in a mental health clinic, and he's okay with that. There's a chance we can make this work, that I could get visiting rights with Bailey.

But it's not the truth.

I need to be completely honest with Grant if I want him to trust me with his daughter, let alone try to establish the connection we had yesterday.

I open my mouth to speak, to tell him the rest of my terrible truth, when there's a wail from the back seat.

Bailey's awake, and she's not happy about it.

"Hello princess," Grant coos. "Do you need a diaper change before our hike?"

He gets out of the car and retrieves her from the backseat, seeing to her needs like a pro.

The moment is gone, and any truth I was going to confess to Grant is lost. He thinks I was in a clinic dealing with my mental health, and that's how we'll have to leave it.

7
GRANT

Bailey giggles as April chases her through the undergrowth. She's got muddy smudges on her rainbow tights from where my little girl keeps falling over, still unsteady on her feet. But every time, she picks herself up and keeps running.

April ducks behind a pine tree and Bailey stops, grasping the huge trunk to clamber over the roots. April moves around behind the large pine, and Bailey gives a surprised shriek when she's not where she thought she was going to be.

April pops out from behind the trunk, and Bailey laughs a deep belly laugh that has her falling backwards and landing with a thud amongst the leaves.

They both laugh and I laugh too, watching them play.

April is a natural with her niece and Bailey's taken to her easily, making me wonder if she remembers her aunt.

April's confession as to why she wasn't around when Bailey needed her has softened my feelings toward her. Mental health isn't something easy to deal with. I want to ask more about it, but I don't want to ruin the carefree mood of the day.

It's getting late in the afternoon, and I begin to pack up the picnic so we can head back.

I've gotten to know April better. We talked easily during the hike and over lunch. And seeing her with Bailey makes me realize I can't ignore her. Not that I want to. I'm mesmerized by the woman.

When she's playing with her niece, the dark circles and haunted look disappear. She's got to be at least ten years younger than me, but she's stirring up emotions inside me that make me feel like a younger man.

I want her.

There's no denying my feelings.

But she's Bailey's aunt. I shouldn't go there. And if she's been unwell, April's vulnerable.

She picks Bailey up and twirls the little girl in her arms before resting her on her hip. I'm crouching on the forest floor stuffing the remains of the picnic into my backpack. We're in a clearing in the woods, and a ray of sunshine peeks through the canopy of trees and beams right onto the two of them.

For a moment, it looks like April has a halo. From my position looking up at them, she's bathed in light, her wide smile adding to the glow emanating from her. She has Bailey balanced on her hip, and an image pops into my head of her round with my child in her belly.

Bailey tugs on April's hair, and they both laugh. My baby and my woman.

I must be staring, because April catches my eye.

"Everything okay?" she asks.

I've just had a vision of my future, and you're in it carrying my baby.

I smile softly and shake my head. I can't tell her what my heart knows. It's too soon.

"I'm glad you found us."

Her smile falters, and she looks away quickly and slides Bailey to the ground.

The haunted look is back, and I wonder what I've said to upset her. She's still holding onto secrets. My mysterious April.

I want to know them all. I want her to open up to me so I can take all of her pain.

"Come back and have dinner with me."

Bailey wails to be picked up again, and April slings her into her arms.

"I'd like that."

As she carries my baby out of the forest, I'm not sure if she's coming to dinner because she wants to spend more time with Bailey or if she's coming for me.

8
APRIL

My heart thumps louder every time Grant sets down a dish before me.

We spent an amazing day together. I got to know my silly niece and also the mischievous man who's her father.

I helped bathe Bailey and put her to bed, and now we're sitting at the dining table while Grant serves up spaghetti bolognaise.

"You want a glass of wine?"

My mouth goes dry at the thought of wine. But I don't trust myself to drink. Not yet. It's too soon.

"I'd prefer soda if you have one?"

He brings me a can of soda and thankfully doesn't ask any questions about why I don't drink. My back's acting up after the walk today, and I rub it absentmindedly.

"What happened to your back?" Grant asks.

I pull my hand away from my lower back.

"It's an injury that acts up sometimes."

He sips his beer. "Oh yeah? What happened?"

I've been rolling a coil of spaghetti around my fork and I stuff it into my mouth now, giving me time to think while I chew.

I hate talking about the accident. It brings up so many bad memories, not of the actual accident but of what happened after. It's the exact moment I can pinpoint when my life got turned upside down, and everything spiraled out of control from there.

"I was ice skating."

Grant raises an eyebrow. "You like to skate?" He seems excited, and I guess living in the mountains means he's an outdoorsy person.

Like the person I used to be.

"I haven't skated since the accident."

He frowns at me. "I'm sorry. There's awesome skating here in the winter."

A pang of regret pierces my chest. I used to ice skate and hike and do fun stuff until the darkness took over and changed everything.

"So what happened? It must have been a bad fall."

I swallow my mouthful. "It was. I was with Karen and some friends. She'd been drinking, which isn't a great idea when ice skating. She pulled me out onto the ice and was all wobbly. There was a frozen island in the middle of the lake, and she had her back to it. She spun me around too fast and let go. I crashed into the barrier and landed on my back against a tree."

"Ouch." He winces.

"Yeah, it was an unfortunate angle. I had a spinal fracture."

"You broke your back?" He looks shocked, and I'm used to this reaction.

I couldn't believe it myself when the doctor told me. The pain made me pass out, and I came to in an ambulance with Karen clasping my hand. Tears were streaming down her face, and she was whispering, *"I'm so sorry,"* over and over.

"I needed surgery, then a back brace."

His gaze is pure concern. "I'm so sorry. That must have been painful."

I swallow another mouthful. If I'd been stronger, if I'd put up with the pain, things might have been different.

"The recovery took a long time. I had chronic pain for months."

"I'm so sorry." Grant's looking at me with pity in his gaze, and I drink it in. This is the good part of my story. The part where I'm the wronged sister garnering all the sympathy.

"I didn't speak to Karen for months. I blamed her for the accident."

Which was stupid. If I'd known my days with my sister were numbered, I would have forgiven her sooner. So much wasted time.

I take a gulp of soda, because thinking about all of this really has me wanting something stronger. Karen had been reckless ever since our parents passed. I was the sensible one who kept her in check. I was always telling her to slow down, to drink less, to respect her body more. I was furious when her antics got me stuck in a hospital bed for nine months.

It was only when she called with the news that she was pregnant that I saw her again. Bailey was born a few months later. But by then, I was the reckless one.

But I'm not ready to tell Grant all of this. He's been looking at me all day like he wants me, like he's interested in me, like I'm someone worth spending time with. And it's been a long time since anyone looked at me like that.

Not to mention the way my body's responding. Every time he's near, my knees go weak and my core tightens. He's awakened something inside me that I thought had died in my accident.

"How about you? How did you end up halfway up a mountain?"

The subject change isn't lost on Grant. I've given him all I can for now. The wounds are still too fresh, and if I keep talking, they might crack open.

Besides, if he knew all of my story, he'd probably chuck me out of his house. And the more time I spend time with Grant, the more I crave him.

It's not just about Bailey now. I'm developing feelings for this man.

We talk easily for the rest of dinner, and Grant tells me about his life on the mountain but little about the military.

I'm not the only one with demons. Grant skirts around his experiences in the military but talks for hours about his bikes and the MC he's a part of. They sound like good guys, and it makes me wistful thinking about the way they treated me last night, like I was part of a family. I wonder if I'll ever have that. A family of my own.

"Penny for them?"

I'm snapped back to the present by Grant's question.

I'm helping him with the washing up, and my hands are in the sink as I stare out the window at the dark forest. Grant's looking at me curiously with a half-smile. In the dim evening light, the flecks in his hair shine silver and make him look even more handsome than in the daylight.

My body trembles at how close he is.

"Um, I was just thinking about going home."

His expression darkens, and he drops the dishcloth he's holding on the counter. "When do you need to be back?"

I lower my eyes. I haven't told him that I walked out on my job. That I left everything in West Virginia, because if I stayed, I was scared I'd get pulled back to the darkness.

That I didn't have any other plan than coming here, connecting with my niece, and saving her from the bad man I imagined him to be.

"I've got a few more days." It's not a complete lie, but it still feels like acid in my throat. He's looking at me intensely and with such raw emotion that I catch my breath.

"You can stay here."

For a moment I think he's asking me to stay permanently, but that would be stupid. I've only just met him. He can't mean that. He must just mean while I'm here.

"Thank you."

He takes a step closer, and his breath caresses my cheek. I turn my head to him, and our gazes meet.

Then his lips are on mine, firm and warm and sending tendrils of white heat through my body.

Our bodies move together, and I pull my hands out of the sink. He takes them in his and puts them around his waist, not caring that I'm dripping water everywhere.

His body pushes into mine until I'm up against the sink, moving my hips against his. The power of him has my core aching and he lifts my hips up, balancing me on the edge of the sink and sending water cascading over the edge.

It splashes on the floor, and that seems to break the spell. Grant steps back, and a look of regret crosses his face.

"I'm sorry."

Disappointment stabs at my heart. I want him to kiss me again. I want to get lost in his heat and feel the solidness of him against me. I want his realness, the first good and true thing I've felt in months.

"Don't be sorry."

He takes another step back. "You're vulnerable, and I'm taking advantage."

Confusion clouds my brain until I remember our conversation in the woods. He thinks I've had mental health problems; he thinks that's what I've been dealing with.

"It's okay." I shake my head. "It's not what you think."

He runs a hand through his hair.

"You don't have to tell me, April. But if you're dealing with depression or something like that, then I won't take advantage of you."

Damn him and his honorable intentions. I want him to rip my clothes off. I want to feel something real with him.

But if I want that, then I need to tell him the truth. He deserves that from me.

"Mental health isn't the reason I couldn't be Bailey's guardian."

His brow furrows. "I thought that's what you said…"

"Well, it is kind of, I guess. But it's more complicated than that…"

I run my hands through my hair and blow out a long breath. Now that it's time to confess, I'm not sure where to begin. He'll kick me out once he knows, and there'll be no more seeing Bailey. But I can't go further with Grant without telling the truth.

With regret I take a deep breath, ready to talk, but he cuts me off.

"You don't need to tell me, April. Not yet. Whatever it is, it's clear it's painful for you to talk about."

I nod. "It is. But…"

"Na-ah." He shakes his head. "I don't want to cause you any more pain tonight, April. You can tell me tomorrow."

Relief floods me. I've got a free pass. I've got one night before Grant learns the truth, and I don't intend to waste it.

"Okay." I take a step closer to him so our bodies brush together, and he groans. "You're not taking advantage of me, Grant. I want you. I can't explain it, but I want you." I say it simply and hope he reads the truth in my eyes.

He smiles. "Let me ease your troubles, April. You're a woman who needs a release. Let me take away your worries for a night and make you feel good. We can talk tomorrow."

I should tell him no; I shouldn't let this go further until we've talked. But his words pull at a longing in my soul. All the pent up anxiety from the last few years aches for release.

Now I'm the one taking advantage of him. But the selfish part of me wants to. To have one night to enjoy this man, one night before he finds out the truth.

Then his lips are on mine, and all thoughts flee my mind. There's nothing but his mouth and his heat and the press of his solid weight against mine.

9
GRANT

April's body pressed against mine feels like heaven. Her lips are soft and pliant as I kiss her long and hard. I've been waiting for this moment ever since I saw her on the side of the road. It was inevitable that we would end up here. It just took longer than it should've because I was blindsided by who she was.

But none of that matters when I feel her hips grind against mine.

She's the woman who's supposed to be in my arms, and that's all that matters. Whatever happened in her past, whatever she's dealing with, I'll work through it with her.

There's hurt in this woman's past, and I'll be the one to soothe her. April is mine now, and I'll find a way to make her whole.

"Follow me." I take her hand and lead her to the bedroom. We creep quietly past Bailey's room, but she's sleeping soundly.

Once I get April in my room, I slowly undress her, taking my time with each item of clothing and kissing every new part of her that's exposed.

Her creamy skin gets goose pimples under my touch, and she sighs contentedly as I move my lips down her throat to nip at her breasts. Her nipples form hard peaks and I suck one into my mouth, making her gasp.

The sound has my cock aching for her, but I need to look after her first.

"I'm going to take care of you," I tell her. "Lie back and let me release whatever's got you so wound up."

She gives me a shy smile and does as she's told, lying back on the bed and spreading her thighs for me.

Her swollen lips part and I get the first glimpse of her beautiful pearl, ripe and ready to be sucked. My mouth kisses her thighs and moves upwards to her sweet swollen lips.

She tastes sweet and musky, and the way her pussy quivers at every kiss makes my cock throb for her.

She's so sensitive it makes me wonder if she's

experienced at all. I don't like the thought of another man touching my girl, but I have to know.

"Have you done this before, April?" She sits up on her elbows, and I'm pleased to note some of the tiredness is gone from her eyes.

"No," she whispers. "I'm a virgin."

The words make my cock sing. I'll be the first and the last to touch her virgin pussy. This is a claiming right here, and my cock and my heart ache for it.

But first I want to see her lose control on the tip of my tongue. I want her to come so hard she forgets whatever's troubling her. I want her body to be so exhausted that she falls into a deep, dreamless sleep.

I dip my head between her legs and lick her juicy folds as I spread her cream around with my finger. She moans delicately and I slide a finger inside, making her gasp. She claps a hand over her mouth.

"You can make some noise, April."

"I don't want to wake the baby."

I chuckle. "Bailey will sleep through anything. The burglar alarm got tripped the other night, and she slept right through it."

April seems to relax.

"So unless you're going to scream louder than my alarm, we're good."

She lies back on the bed, and I watch her as I

slide a second finger into her tight cunt. She cries out, not afraid to make some noise this time, and the sound has my cock throbbing.

I dip my head between her thighs. I want to make her cum before I let myself loose on her. My tongue flicks her hard bundle of nerves, and she trembles with every touch.

With my fingers pumping in and out of her, I slowly press harder with my tongue until she's writhing under me. Her legs wrap around my head, and she pushes her hips into my face.

I love it that she feels safe enough with me to lose control.

Her pussy gushes and her thighs clamp around my head as the orgasm thunders through her body. She pushes herself onto me and I grip her ass, holding her in place while she comes.

I only give her a moment to enjoy the high before I lick her again, chasing another orgasm with my hungry mouth.

Once she's come down from the second orgasm, I crawl onto the bed with her. I want to flip her over and pull apart her wide ass cheeks, but something tells me to go gentle.

April needs to be cared for, because it's plain to me that she hasn't had tenderness in her life lately.

There'll be plenty of time to explore all of my

woman and fuck her every way possible, but for tonight, I roll her onto her side so our bodies are as close as they can be.

Our eyes meet, and hers are hooded with desire. There's no tension, no tiredness. Her skin is glowing with perspiration and she smiles at me, looking fresh and youthful like she should.

"Hey you."

"Hey you." I grin right back at her.

My heart soars for this woman. She's crashed into my life, and it feels so damn right. Despite the circumstances, despite the age gap, despite everything. We're right where we're meant to be, in my bed with our bodies entwined.

I kiss her gently and then deepen the kiss as she responds.

My cock presses against her thigh and she opens her legs, giving me access. The tip of my dick slides between her slick lips, but I pause.

Now that I'm a dad, I can't wait to grow my family, and I'd love to put a baby in April's belly. But it's a lot for April to take in all at once. Whatever happened after her accident, whatever state of mind it put her in, she needs time to find herself. To erase the worry lines and dark circles permanently before we add to our family.

I reach for a condom from the side drawer, but she stops my hand.

"I'm on the pill," she says shyly, "To balance my hormones. Are you clean?"

"I'm clean, and I haven't been with anyone for a long time." Those days for me are long gone. And now I've found my woman. She's all I need.

"I want to feel all of you, Grant."

The words make pre-cum leak from my dick. "I want to feel all of you too, April. Nothing between us."

A shadow falls briefly across her face, and then it's gone so quick I think I imagined it. She's probably just nervous about her first time. A reminder for me to take it slow.

"I'll take care of you, April. It might hurt a little, but only for a moment."

She nods quickly, and then her lips find mine. There's a new hunger in her kiss, a determination that makes my blood heat.

I deepen the kiss and our bodies slide together, slick with sweat. I hook her thigh over mine and adjust my hips to find her silky entrance.

Emotion flows out of me as my tip slides into April. I've never felt this close to anyone, this connected, and the feeling wraps around my heart and my chest, filling my insides with warmth. I can't put it into words, and I don't want to scare her away with the intensity of my feelings. Instead, I show her how I feel with my body.

Grabbing her hips, I slowly slide my cock inside her sticky entrance, and her pussy envelopes me in delicious wet heat. The sensations course up my body and have me groaning like a wild animal.

She gasps, and her eyes widen. I leave one hand on her hip and lock the other with mine.

My gaze latches to hers and we stare at each other with wonder as I slowly ease inside her until I come up against her virgin barrier.

April winces, and I pause.

"Breathe with me."

She keeps her eyes locked with mine and our hands entwined, breathing deeply as I thrust through her virgin walls.

She cries out and her face scrunches up in a grimace, and she squeezes my hand till the knuckles turn white.

I catch her pain with a kiss, pausing my cock inside her until she relaxes.

I'll always catch her pain; I want all of her troubles unloaded onto me. I'll spend the rest of my life soothing this girl any way I can.

When I feel her relax, I move slowly, tilting her

hips until we find a slow rhythm, our bodies finding the places where they fit together.

It's the slowest, sweetest sex I've ever had. Emotion threatens to overwhelm me and I grasp April's hand hard, needing her to anchor me as much as she needs me.

I kiss her throat and her breasts, and our slow dance quickens as the need for release grows inside me.

My hand finds her clit, and I rub circles until she's moaning into my mouth. She clasps my ass with a new urgency and grinds her hips against mine, and I feel the pressure building inside her. The pressure on her clit intensifies as I help her find her release. When her pussy convulses around me, I hold on, not wanting to finish yet, not ready to end this.

The trembling in her body ceases, and I kiss her sweaty brow.

"Good girl."

She smiles at me, but I'm not done with her yet. I want to go deeper; I want to feel all of her.

I roll April onto her back and bend her leg to her chest. My dick slides deep into her pussy, and she cries out as I fill her right up.

My balls slap her asshole and I thrust hard, loving the way her breasts jiggle with every slam of my cock.

Her hands grab my ass and she grinds me against her clit every time I thrust into her, moving her hips to meet my thrusts.

"Just there…"

She whimpers and I slam into her, pounding her hard to hit her spot. I love watching her face as she reaches her climax, and this time I let myself go with her. I let the wave of emotion wash over me as I explode inside April.

Any last doubts about her release with me. In this moment we're joined, and there's nothing in this world that could change the way I feel about her.

We collapse on the bed together. Hair sticks to April's forehead in sweating curls, and I gently brush it off her face.

Her eyes flutter closed, and her breathing gets heavy.

"I love you," I whisper. But she's already fast asleep.

10

GRANT

I wake up the next morning to the harsh ring of my phone. The sheets are tangled, and it takes me a moment to locate it in the back pocket of my jeans that are still on the floor where April tugged them off last night.

Memories of last night flood my brain, and I smile to myself as I scramble for my phone. April isn't in the bed, and she must have gotten up already.

I haven't heard Bailey yet either, which is a relief. I love it when my daughter sleeps in.

I curse as I finally locate my phone, because it's just after seven, and whoever's calling better have a damn good excuse.

It's Tabitha, my case worker from the agency that connected me with Bailey. She's kept in touch to make sure I'm settling into fatherhood and that

Bailey is well cared for. She's the one who first told me April was back and looking for custody.

This is good timing. I can tell her that we've worked it out, that April isn't a monster, just an aunt wanting a piece of her family, and if I have my way, she'll be staying here permanently.

"Morning."

"Grant," Tabitha barks, which has me sitting up straighter. She's usually mild-mannered and calm, and I've never heard her raise her voice.

"April's skipped town. We think she might be heading your way to try to take Bailey."

I can't help the chuckle that escapes my lips. They've got April down as some bad guy when all she wants is what's best for her niece.

"She's here already."

Tabitha sucks in her breath. "You mean you've seen her?"

I've done a lot more than see her. I've tasted her and heard her moan.

"Yes, she's…"

Tabitha cuts me off. "Whatever you do, don't let her near Bailey."

There's panic in her voice, and I'm not used to that with Tabitha. She's been nothing but kind. She was wary of me at first because she wanted to do what was best for Bailey. She'll always put the child first. So if she's panicking there's a damn good reason for it.

A kernel of doubt unfurls in my stomach.

"Why?"

What am I missing?

"She's desperate, Grant. I couldn't tell you before because of confidentiality, but the situation has changed. April's a junkie."

"A junkie?"

Time stands still for a long heartbeat, and my stomach drops.

She can't be talking about April. About the kind, curvy woman I've gotten to know.

"That's why she didn't get custody. She's an addict and was known to the authorities…"

I don't hear the rest of what Tabitha says. It makes sense. The dark rings under her eyes, the troubled look, the secrets she was keeping, the way she rubs her hands up and down her thighs when she gets anxious.

But can April really be an addict? She's been nothing but sweet and kind and gentle. I can't marry the picture of a drug addict with the curvy woman who's in my house.

She's in my house. She's alone with Bailey.

I race out of bed, almost tripping in the bed sheets, and tear down the hall to Bailey's room.

The crib is empty.

Panic bolts through my veins, and I spin around and run out of the room.

"Bailey!" I call. But there's no answering giggle.

"April!"

The house is silent, and I stand in the living room butt naked as fear grips my heart. Baby toys are strewn over the rug, but my daughter isn't here.

Panic clenches my stomach, and a fear worse than anything I experienced in Iraq crushes my chest.

Where is my daughter?

A giggle has me racing to the window, and that's when I see them.

April is crouched at the bottom of the slide while Bailey sits at the top. She pushes herself off and gives a happy squeal as she zooms down the slide. April catches her at the bottom, and they both giggle as April hoists her into the air.

I storm out of the house, not caring that I'm naked. The closest neighbors are half a mile away.

"Give me my daughter."

The smile on Aprils face drops when she sees me, but I only have eyes for my daughter.

11
APRIL

The door slams shut, and I jerk my gaze to the house.

Grant thunders down the stairs with his fists clenched and a face so red he might explode.

He knows.

My heart drops into my stomach. Somehow, he's discovered the truth. It doesn't matter how; he knows, and it's over.

He knows the truth about me, and any chance I had with Bailey and with him is gone.

The pain in my chest is so severe it feels like I'm being stabbed in the heart. I knew this was coming, but the anger on his features cleaves my heart in two.

Somehow, I thought last night might make things different. The connection we shared and the mind blowing sex that was like nothing I've ever experienced before. I was going to tell him the truth today, and I stupidly hoped he might understand.

But one look at Grant's lined brow and clenched fists has my heart breaking. He knows, and it's over.

Grant's not bothered to get dressed and even though his anger is turned on me, my gaze takes in his muscular body, covered in tattoos and scars, and his impressive length swinging between his legs.

At least we had last night.

I scoop Bailey up, and as I carry her to her dad, I give her a kiss on the top of her head, burying my face in her soft curls and savoring her milky scent.

"Goodbye, sweet girl."

I hold her out to their father, and he takes her from my arms. Relief floods his face, and he holds her so tight that she squirms.

"I'll get my things." I walk past him and into the house.

There's no point trying to explain myself. I hate myself for what I am, and there's no reasonable explanation for my addiction. For the darkness that took me after the accident. The prescription painkillers that dried up once my insurance ran out, but not without first taking their hold on me. The strong opioids that got me through back surgery and recovery but left me reliant on them and addicted to their warmth and the golden glow they surrounded me with. The clawing feeling when I didn't have them. The way my skin itched and my back ached and my insides burnt so intensely that I had to find a substitute on the street.

A "friend" introduced me to Fentanyl. He gave me a pill, and it was no different to the prescription opioids I'd been on. At least that's what I told myself. No different.

Except it was different. It was stronger, and more addictive, and illegal.

Somehow, it's okay for my doctor to prescribe me opioids and leave me addicted, but if I try to feed that addiction on the street, I'm nothing but a junkie. Another statistic of the West Virginia opioid epidemic.

I head into the house and grab my backpack from the living room. I'm zipping it up when I hear Grant come into the room behind me.

He sets Bailey down on her play mat and she gets busy pushing large colorful beads around a metal loop.

"Why didn't you tell me?"

I pick up my bag and shoulder it.

"Would it have made a difference? I got one night with you and a day with Bailey. At least I got that."

He's frowning at me.

"Where are you going?"

"I'm leaving. You obviously know, somehow, about what I am. So I'm leaving before you kick me out."

Grant looks at me, and he shakes his head slowly. "I'm not kicking you out, April."

He says it gently, and it takes me a moment to register what he's really saying.

"I'm mad because you didn't tell me. You didn't trust me."

There's hurt in his eyes and genuine concern.

"I tried to. But it's hard to admit that you're a former addict.'

He cocks his head. "Former?"

"I've been clean for eight weeks, three days, and seven hours."

It comes out bitter, because I'm still at the stage where every hour feels like a victory. Where the days stretch long ahead of me, and each one I get through without using is an achievement.

"Is that where you were when Karen had the accident? Were you in rehab?"

I shake my head, ashamed to admit that when Karen had the accident I was trying to hold down a waitressing job doing double shifts, so I could afford the Fentanyl that I needed to get through each day.

Karen was so frightened of my addiction that the

last time we saw each other we argued, and she told me she didn't want me around her daughter. But it wasn't until her death, until I lost her and then wasn't considered a suitable guardian for Bailey, that I became determined to kick the darkness for good no matter what.

"I went into rehab after Karen passed. When I realized I was going to lose my niece, lose the only family I had left."

I hang my head, ashamed of what I was. Ashamed that the addiction got ahold of me so easily. I thought I was strong. I had survived the loss of my parents as a child, but my therapist helped me realize that that childhood trauma may have helped fan the addiction.

Grant strides across the room, and his hand cups my chin.

"Look at me when we're talking. There's nothing to be ashamed of."

I look into his eyes, not daring to hope that he might understand. That he might see me as something other than an addict.

"You don't want me to go? You aren't worried about me being around Bailey?" It comes out as a whisper because my throat is clogged with emotion.

Grant shakes his head. "No, April. Addiction is a

sickness. It's something you fight and recover from. It's not a reason to give up on someone."

Emotion overwhelms me, and I crumple against him. It's more than I deserve, that this man understands the fight I've been through, that I still battle with every time my back hurts or something makes me anxious.

"Talk to me, April. Tell me everything. No more secrets."

Grant makes me a coffee, and we talk for a long time.

I tell him everything. The prescribed painkillers and then the ones I got on the street. The addiction that left me worn out and exhausted but craving the next hit. Knowing I needed to kick the habit but never quite being able to. The waiting lists on the programs, so that every time I thought I was making progress, there wouldn't be enough funding for the next round.

Then the unexpected inheritance from Karen. Money from our parents that she'd never told me about. Half of it was hers and went to Bailey, but the other half was mine.

I used some of the money to get private help. To get into a good rehab center and get the therapy I needed to kick the addiction.

But it didn't help me get the one thing I wanted. I

thought I'd be able to turn up and get custody of Bailey, that Grant would be happy to hand her over to another relative. But the authorities saw my record. I was caught once with Fentanyl, and now I'm forever a junkie in the system, marked as an addict.

Grant listens to it all quietly, occasionally shaking a toy for Bailey and picking her up when she starts to whine.

He puts her down for her morning nap and I slouch on the sofa, my body suddenly tired. I feel exhausted but free. Talking about it is the best therapy, and whatever happens now, at least Grant knows my truth.

When Grant comes back into the room, he sits next to me on the couch.

"What help do you need to get better?" He takes my hands in his and warmth spreads from them, reviving my tired bones. "Whatever you need, April, I'm here for you. You've got family now. Me and Bailey. If you want to stay here with me, that is."

Happy tears sting my eyes, because it's too much to hope for.

"You mean it?"

"I love you, April. I want you here, and I'll do whatever it takes to help you stay on the right path."

His words are a balm to my soul. Just having him

here and having his support feels like enough. But if I'm going to beat this for good, I need to give myself the best chance.

"Honestly, I'm not sure. I think keeping up the therapy will help. But being here with you in the mountains is already helping. Doing things like hiking again, ice skating, getting a job will help. I don't know if the addiction will ever take hold of me again, Grant. I honestly don't know."

His hand cups my cheeks. "We'll work through it, honey. Whatever comes up, I'm here for you. And not just me. You wanted family, you've got an entire MC now. We'll support you in any way we can."

I swipe at my eyes, and my chest swells. For the first time there's no restlessness, no craving for anything other than what I have right here before me.

A warm glow spreads around me, and the air seems to hum. It feels like I'm high, but this one is all natural.

I've got the love of a good man and I've got my niece. I've got family, and I've got love. It's better than any synthetic high could ever provide.

EPILOGUE

APRIL

Eighteen months later…

"Have you tried cutting the afternoon nap short? It may be that he's getting too much sleep." Trish has one baby on her hip while she feeds Rose, her eldest, a piece of toast in her highchair.

Kendra paces the kitchen with Ruben pressed to her shoulder. She's got dark circles under her eyes and her hand moves mechanically, rubbing Ruben's back as she tries to soothe his cries.

Bailey is in the corner with Bettie, Danni's little girl, and I keep one eye on them as I slice the tomatoes for the salad.

"I don't like to wake him," says Kendra. "I'm usually napping too."

There are murmurs of recognition from the women in the room. Ruben's been a terrible sleeper ever since he was born, and toddlerhood hasn't changed anything.

I rub my belly with a smile.

It will be a few months yet before we welcome our little girl into the world, and I can't wait for her to join the extended family.

"Should I do two apple pies or just the one?" Maggie asks. "Two," I say at the same time as Danni and Trish and we all laugh.

It's the monthly club dinner tonight, and the restaurant has closed so we have free rein of the kitchen. There's roast meat in the smoker out back, and the women are in the kitchen doing the salads and side dishes.

"Why don't you go have a lie down now?" Danni takes the fussy toddler off Kendra, and she gives her a grateful look.

"Thank you. I might do that."

Kendra heads out of the kitchen, and we resume our work preparing the meal. It's one big family here, and we look out for each other.

Bailey calls every woman in this room aunt, and I'm aunty to every child here too. We help each other when needed and have each other's back. I know when my time comes in a few months that my MC sisters will be looking out for me too.

I took a waitressing job in the Wild Taste Restaurant and Bar, which has helped me stay focused on my recovery. A few months ago, I started studying part time for a degree in psychology. I want to help others like me to beat addiction.

Trish has just opened a refuge center for women, and I help out there a few times a week. We see women coming through who have addiction issues or are fleeing situations with them. I want to do more to help, and once I have my degree and certifications, I'll work with Trish full-time.

I've never once slipped up, and as the months pass, it becomes easier and easier. I look back on those dark times as if they happened to another person. It doesn't feel like that was me.

Every day I'm grateful that Grant gave me a chance. With his support and the MC, I'm a different person, one who's able to cope with life's ups and downs.

The door bursts open, and my heart flutters when I see it's Grant. He's got a mischievous smile on his face, and his glance goes first to Bailey and then to me.

"April." He raises his eyebrows. "I need your help for a minute."

I glance at Maggie and she raises her eyebrows. "Go," she says. "I'll finish the salad."

I wipe my hands, wondering what it is that I'm needed for. Although when I see the mischievous glint in Grant's eye, I've got a pretty good idea.

"Will you keep an eye on Bailey for us?" Grant asks Danni.

"Of course."

She raises her eyebrows at me. "Have fun," she mouths.

The girls giggle as the door closes behind us.

Grant slides his arm around my waist and rests it on my belly. Since we found out I was pregnant, he doesn't like to let me out of his sight for long.

"What do you need help with?"

He takes my hand and slides it between his legs to the hard bulge in his jeans.

"With this."

He nips at my ear, and heat courses through my veins. My pussy gushes, and my core pulls up tight. Since I entered the second trimester, I've been horny as hell, and one touch from my husband has me all wet.

He pushes me against the wall and captures my mouth in a passionate kiss. My hips grind against his, and he grabs my ass and pulls me toward him.

A door slamming has us jumping apart. Prez

strides toward us down the corridor that leads out to the back entrance.

I giggle at being caught, but the laughter dies in my throat when I see his face. Prez's brows are knit together, and a scowl creases his weathered features. There's someone trailing behind him, and it's not till he gets closer that I see he's holding the hand of a woman. Or more like dragging her down the hall. She has to jog to keep up with his long strides, but he's not slowing down.

Prez looks up at Grant, and his scowl increases.

"You didn't see her."

I frown at his words, but Grant's eyes go wide when he sees the woman.

She's young, probably younger than me, but it's hard to tell with her face full of makeup. She's got thick, dark hair that shimmers in the light of the corridor.

"I'll explain later," Prez barks at Grant's questioning look.

He leads the woman through to the meeting room and shuts the door firmly behind them.

Grant stares after them, his eyebrows still raised in shock.

"What has he gotten himself into?" he mutters. "This will bring nothing but trouble to the club."

"Who was that?" I ask.

Grant's still staring at the closed door with his brow furrowed.

"That was Isabella Berone. Carlo Berone's daughter."

The name makes me shiver. I've heard Carlo mentioned around the club. He's the head of a criminal family that operates on the mountains.

"I didn't know the club was involved in their business."

From what I've learned, the Wild Riders MC is legit. They don't do anything illegal.

"We aren't," says Grant. "I hope Prez isn't about to do anything stupid." He shakes his head slowly. "I guess we'll find out soon enough."

He turns his attention back to me and slides his arm around my waist. "Now, where were we?"

"I believe I was about to help you with a little problem."

My hand snakes to his bulge, and I give him a squeeze through his jeans.

"Hey, it's a big problem, sweetheart."

I giggle, and Grant snatches up my hand. We take the stairs two at a time, heading for the rooms upstairs. The first room is empty, and Grant locks the door behind us.

His hands are all over me before I get a chance to turn around. I arch my back into him, and he runs his hands down my throat and over my breasts. One hand stays on my breast, and he slides the other between my legs.

"I want you, April, so bad."

I grind my ass into him to let him know I feel the same.

His hands on me set my skin on fire, and I don't turn around but keep my back to him as he maneuvers me toward the middle of the room. There's a chair at the end of the bed, and when we reach it I grab hold of the back of it and press my hips backwards.

He groans as I grind against him, and my panties gush wet heat.

His lips move over my neck, and his deft fingers pull my skirt up. Then his hands are yanking my panties to the side, and his fingers run over my wet folds.

I moan as his touch penetrates me and bend right over to give him full access. The sound of his zipper undoing has another wave of heat racing through me, and then I feel his cock slither between my legs.

I raise onto my tiptoes as he finds my entrance and slams home. The jolt has me slamming into the chair and I brace myself, gripping hard as my husband takes what's his.

I feel every ridge of his cock as he pounds my

pussy, making me bounce around like a rag doll on the end of his cock.

His hand finds its way into my bra, and he pulls the bra down to grab one breast. With his hand on my tit and the other on my hip, he bucks into me, ploughing me hard and rough and making the heat pool in my belly as he hits my g-spot.

"I'm gonna come," I moan as the pressure builds.

"Good girl. Come for me, April," he grunts between gritted teeth. It's raw and fast, and the pure need he has for me tips me over the edge.

I cry out as waves of pleasure engulf me. My pussy convulses, sucking his cock into me as I come. Then he stiffens and releases and hot cum floods my pussy.

He pulls me to him, holding me in place by the hips so my pussy milks every last drop from him.

We're both breathing hard when Grant gently puts my panties back in place and smooths my skirt down.

Only then do I turn around and kiss my husband. He takes me in his arms, and I'm surrounded by warmth and good feelings.

My husband is still the best high I've ever had.

* * *

BONUS SCENE

Haven't had enough of Grant and April? Find out what family life looks like at the ice skating lake.

Read the bonus scene when you sign up to the Sadie King mailing list.

To sign up visit:
authorsadieking.com/bonus-scenes

Already a subscriber? Check your last email for the link to access all the bonus content.

WHAT TO READ NEXT

She's off-limits and half his age, but this ex-military biker is a protector hero who won't give up the woman who captures his heart.

Isabella Berone has haunted my dreams since I watched her strut into the White Out nightclub two years ago.

She was too young then, the mafia princess with something to prove. But I watched, and I waited.

When Isabella needs me, I'm there for her. I'll protect her with my life. Because despite the age gap, despite her being off limits, I've fallen for the wild mafia princess.

When her father comes for her, I'll be ready. I swore to fight for my country once, and now I'll fight for Isabella, no matter the cost.

Wild Heart is a protector hero, forbidden love, age gap romance featuring the President of an MC and the wild and curvy mafia princess who steals his heart.

WILD HEART

CHAPTER ONE

Raiden

The air is thick with expensive cologne and the smell of fruity cocktails. Pop music blasts from the speakers near the dance floor, making me want to cover my ears and high tail it out of here.

Coming to the White Out isn't my idea of a good time, but it's not every day one of my MC gets married, although it's happening more and more these days. Arlo's in his early thirties and not an old man like me, so when White Out, the club at the Emerald Heart Resort, was suggested for his bachelor party, I agreed that I'd come and not complain about the music.

That was before I got here.

The beat goes way too fast to be comfortable and

the lyrics are shouted rather than sung, making me question the musical ability of the vocalist. Why the hell they can't put on something decent that everyone loves, like Foo Fighters, I don't know. Hell, I'd even go for classic pop. Give me Duran Duran and Madonna over this shit any day.

"Here you go." The bartender slides a tray of shot glasses filled with white liquid at me. I squint at the tray, trying to understand why I've got a tray of tequila shots in front of me.

"I didn't order these."

The bartender smiles nervously, and a bead of sweat glistens on his forehead.

We're not wearing our cuts tonight out of respect to Axel. He's the owner of this joint, and I don't want to bring him any trouble. Not that my boys are trouble. But I've come across the type of entitled hot heads who frequent the Emerald Heart Resort, and an MC patch can attract the wrong kind of attention from those kinds of dickheads.

But even without the jackets, we're pretty imposing. My guys are all ex-military and built for strength. Half the MC have beards and tattoos that dress shirts won't fully cover. Compared to the scrawny rich kids on the dance floor, we stand out. Axel would have clocked us the moment we walked in and no doubt let his staff know the Wild Riders Motorcycle Club are in tonight.

"That guy ordered them..." The bartender licks his lips nervously. "...and he said you were paying." His head tilts to the left, indicating someone further down the bar.

I lean forward to see past a container of brightly colored compostable containers. Arlo gives me one of his trademark wide grins. We don't call him Prince Charming for nothing.

I sigh heavily. I'd rather be at our headquarters drinking craft beer and listening to Van Halen, but it's too early to bail out of Arlo's party. Besides, as the President of the MC I need to make sure my guys have a good time and no one gives us any trouble.

"Set up a tab on this." I pull my credit card from my wallet. "Put anything my boys ask for on there."

The bartender looks at the card uncertainly. His eyes flick upwards to the left hand corner of the bar. I follow his gaze to a security camera attached to the overhang of the bar. Axel keeps his beady eye on everything that goes on at the resort and especially at White Out.

"Clear it with Axel first if you need to."

I don't want to make this young guy feel

awkward for doing his job. I place a hundred dollar bill on the counter. "And look after my boys tonight."

He nods uncertainly but pockets the bill.

I look at the camera and give Axel a wave. Son of a bitch needs to get out more if he's still spending every night behind his bank of monitors.

A new song starts, and there's a whoop from the dance floor. I guess it's better than hanging out down here.

The guys join me at the bar, and Arlo hands out the shots. I knock it back, feeling the burn, and chase it with the beer I just ordered.

That's the last shot I'll have tonight. I'm too old for this shit.

Some of the younger guys head toward the dance floor, and I slide into a booth with Quentin. His huge thighs scrape the underside of the table. That's why we call him Barrels. He's the biggest guy in the MC. That, and the fact that he runs the brewery for the club.

"You not dancing, Prez?" Quentin asks.

"What the fuck do you think?"

He chuckles, and we each sip our beer. It's a prestigious brand that suits the clientele who come here, but it lacks flavor. I can tell Quentin's thinking the same thing by the way he swirls it around in his mouth. When you run a brewery and craft beer bar, you become quite the connoisseur.

Barrels finally swallows, and his face screws up in a wince. "Tastes like piss."

"It's not gonna win any awards, that's for sure."

"Too sweet, tastes like caramel." Quentin holds the bottle up to the light and swishes the brown liquid around. "And the viscosity's too dense."

My younger self would be laughing his ass off if he could see me now. Discussing the taste notes and viscosity of the beer I'm drinking. My younger self was out to get drunk, and that was it. Taste didn't even come into it.

Thank fuck I grew up.

Travis joins us, and him and Quentin start discussing their entry for the state craft beer awards. An award would be great for business and it's an achievement for the guys, validation that they're doing something right.

Validation's important when you're running a team. I want to make my boys feel like they're achieving something.

They're all ex-military, and half of them broken. Not all the boys came out tonight; Lone Star can't stand to be around most people, Spec's PTSD can be triggered by loud noises, and Davis still has a hang up about his hearing aids.

I'm thinking about Davis, the young prospect, as I slowly sip my beer. I should have pushed him more, insisted he come out. It would have done him good to be around a young crowd.

He gave some lame excuse about not wanting to leave his new puppy alone, but we all knew it's because of his loss of hearing. It would have done him good to talk to a pretty girl tonight, give him some confidence. My men are hooking up like we're running a dating agency. There must be a woman for him somewhere.

I'm lost in my thoughts, but I notice the change in the air when she walks in. My head jerks up towards the door, and my breath catches in my chest.

The woman pauses on the threshold of the club, and her thick dark hair, artfully curled, bounces over her exposed shoulders. She's tall like her father and made more so by the six inch heels she's wearing that make her legs look longer. Her red dress ends above the knee, and there's a hint of thick thighs and delicious promises.

My hungry gaze scans her body, taking in every curve. The way the dress cinches in at the waist and the tight bodice pushes her oversized breasts against the fabric, forcing a pillowing cleavage that makes my throat dry.

Her face has a thick coat of makeup covering her already flawless skin. But it's her eyes that have me spellbound. Emerald green. They scan the room taking everything in, intelligent and with a wariness much older than her years.

The music slows as she walks in. That's what it feels like, but maybe it's just me as my heartbeat speeds up and my pulse quickens. Blood thunders through my ears so loudly I can't hear anything.

The air shifts. It parts for her as she struts into the club. Strut is the only word for how she walks. Her delicate beaded purse hangs off her bent elbow, and the two friends she's with totter on their heels to catch up.

Quentin turns to see what I'm staring at, and his mouth drops open.

"Is that...?"

"Isabella Berone." Her name rumbles out of my chest like a growl. The mafia princess whose father has a deadly reputation.

I haven't seen her since she was an adolescent playing at the lake. Her father keeps her tightly guarded, and I can see why.

My dick's hard as stone, and my heart's pounding. I glance around the club, and every other hot blooded man is staring at her. My fists clench under the table, and I'm overcome with an urge to break the heads of every single one of them.

What the hell she's doing out without a security detail I have no idea, but not a single man in here is going to get near her tonight.

"Get the guys," I growl without taking my eyes off Isabella.

She shouldn't be here. She can't be more than eighteen. I'm damn sure her father doesn't know where she is, and it won't go well for any hot headed man who tries to touch her.

But it's not because of her father that I call my guys together. Isabella may only be eighteen, but I'll make damn sure no one gets near her. No one but me.

To keep reading visit:
mybook.to/WRMCWildHeart

BOOKS AND SERIES BY SADIE KING

Wild Heart Mountain

Military Heroes

Wild Riders MC

Mountain Heroes

Temptation

A Runaway Bride for Christmas

A Secret Baby for Christmas

Sunset Coast

Underground Crows MC

Sunset Security

Men of the Sea

Love and Obsession - The Cod Cove Trilogy

His Christmas Obsession

Maple Springs

Small Town Sisters

Candy's Café

All the Single Dads

Men of Maple Mountain

All the Scars we Cannot See

What the Fudge

Fudge and the Firefighter

The Seal's Obsession

His Big Book Stack

For a full list of Sadie King's books check out her website

www.authorsadieking.com

ABOUT THE AUTHOR

Sadie King is a USA Today Best Selling Author of contemporary romance novellas.

She lives in New Zealand with her ex-military husband and raucous young son.

When she's not writing she loves catching waves with her son, running along the beach, and drinking good wine with a book in hand.

Keep in touch when you sign up for her newsletter. You'll snag yourself a free short romance and access to all the bonus content!

authorsadieking.com/bonus-scenes

Printed in Great Britain
by Amazon